THE EDGE

A Story of Grief, Grit and Grace

A Christian Novella

JOSHUA POWELL

Printed Worldwide
First Printing 2025
First Edition 2025

ISBN: 978-2-63166-396-0

10 9 8 7 6 5 4 3 2 1

Interior Book Design by Walt's Book Design
www.waltsbookdesign.com

*For anyone who has ever come back from the edge
or wondered if they could.*

A Note About the Stories of Hope Series

My hope with *The Edge*—and the other novellas I'm developing for the Stories of Hope Series—is to explore the complicated, messy situations that often reflect real life more than we'd like to admit. These fictional stories reveal the transforming love of Christ that is available to everyone, without prejudice.

Even in the darkest or most tangled circumstances, there is hope to be found in Him.

This story is about a man who discovered that hope for himself.

Bottoms Up

The city street was dimly lit by streetlamps glowing through the misting rain. One could barely make out the storefronts on the edge of town, and the hay fields across the street faded into a blur. However, that never kept Craig from taking a moment to process his surroundings. He had no desire to be here, yet inexplicably found himself staring at the old door yet again. Even from several feet away he could make out the uneven layers of black paint, chipped and cracked from the elements. Definitely not a welcoming entrance. It didn't matter what time of day he arrived. It was always dark, and the same song was always playing: Johnny Cash's "Sunday Morning Coming Down." The door never fully shut when the bar owner unlocked the deadbolt, so a trace of light and music leaked outside. Cash's deep voice lamented the tragedy of a Sunday morning hangover every day, multiple times a day.

Craig understood this song of regret; it filled his mind and heart. Like a zombie, he glanced at the flashing neon sign over the door that read "The Edge." An appropriate name given how it sat on the very outskirts of town. A few other signs with the names of common beers served at the bar flashed as well, but otherwise the front of the bar, painted gray with blacked-out windows, was hardly noticeable. The light from a red sign revealed a small pothole puddle in the parking lot. As Craig walked by, he could make out just a hint of his salt-and-pepper hair that needed to be cut, as well as a longer-than-usual beard. A quick glimpse of his eyes, filled with sadness, made him look away. He almost stepped into the puddle to disrupt the reflection, but he remembered that the sole of his brown cowboy boot had a hole, and there was nothing he hated more than a wet sock.

The door opened as he approached it. Strangely enough, there was no one standing there to open it. The place itself was nearly empty. A few people were sitting at the tables and booths that filled the large room. A man and a woman sat close together in a corner booth. The man, not much older than thirty, looked out of place in khaki pants and a dress shirt. The woman next to him, whose head rested on the man's shoulder, wore a tight-fitting green dress. The man shot Craig a stern look. Craig deduced that the woman was not the man's wife. But who was he to judge? So, as he always did, he turned his head away.

A lone biker stood next to a pool table in the back. The man's leather biker gear looked worn out by time and rough riding. As he leaned over the edge of the table to line up the next shot for his solo game, he grimaced in a way that indicated that the old biker was as weary as his gear. An old jukebox lit up orange and green and provided just enough light to reveal a hallway to the restrooms and an old storage closet.

A mechanic in a dirty jumpsuit seated on a stool at one end of the bar exhaled smoke that collected and hung over the bar and tables. The middle-age woman next to him with long brown hair and heavily applied makeup cackled at whatever the mechanic was saying. Behind the bar was Kip the bartender, who was nearly bald and wore a dirty white shirt and a black apron, along with a smile. Kip was cleaning a glass and shot Craig a look that seemed to beckon him to come and take a seat. At the other end of the bar was a man who always caught Craig's eyes. He was a long-haired, dark-complected fellow with a perpetually joyful countenance, which made him look somewhat out of place in a dreary bar. Craig couldn't quite put his finger on it, but of all the people here, he had no desire to speak with any of them, except maybe this man.

But he never could work up the nerve to introduce himself.

Craig dismissed the impulse to speak to him, like he always did. He sat down on the squeaky metal stool and nodded at Kip, who placed a shot glass of whiskey in front of him. At this point, Craig didn't even want to drink the whiskey. It was all part of some twisted, unavoidable routine. He looked down at the pants pocket of his faded blue jeans where he'd put his cell phone, which was certain to ring at any moment. It always did. He tried to redirect his focus. He looked up and stared for a moment at the bottles on the shelves. Then he focused on the words of the Cash song still playing, letting Cash's deep voice calm his mind a little.

It almost worked. He almost forgot what was coming, but the phone in his pocket shook as it vibrated. Then came the familiar ringtone of an old-fashioned rotary phone. It hurt something deep inside of Craig. He took a deep breath and tried not to cry as he reached into his pocket and pulled it out, almost against his own will. As he raised the phone to his ear, he pressed the answer button.

"Hello," Craig responded.

"Is this Mr. Craig Brown?" the voice replied.

"Yes," Craig muttered.

"I'm Officer Thomas with the police department. There's been an accident, Mr. Craig. Is Mrs. Tabatha Brown your wife?" the voice asked.

"She is," Craig said. "Is she okay?"

He knew the answer to the question, and he wasn't sure why he asked, but he did.

"No, sir," the police officer said firmly but sympathetically. "I'm sorry, but she was killed when an eighteen-wheeler merged into her lane earlier this evening. When we arrived on the site, she had already passed. I'm so sorry. I want you to know—"

Craig hung up the phone. He didn't need to hear anything else. He downed the whiskey, let it burn as it went down his throat, then he closed his eyes as the Johnny Cash song ended.

"Come on, please," Craig uttered to no one in particular. He took a few deep breaths and then opened his eyes. Suddenly, Craig found himself somewhere else: a construction site. The smell of steel, sweat, and freshly laid cement filled his nostrils. As a gust of wind blew by, dirt from the ground flew up and settled on his arm. An orange vest covered the shirt he was wearing, and the hard hat moved slightly as he turned to survey his surroundings.

"Come on, Brown!" He heard a voice yelling at him. Craig turned to see his boss, the foreman, motioning for him to come over and look at a set of plans.

"I'm coming," Craig responded as he walked over from where he was standing and approached a plastic table with a set of plans on it, surrounded by six men.

"You've got to stay with us, Brown. Quit day-dreaming," his foreman said with aggravation in his voice.

Craig nodded his head in agreement and did his best to listen as his foreman began to discuss a recent change made to the project.

He made his way to his old gray Camry along with Jeff, one of his coworkers who had asked for a ride home.

"Thanks again," Jeff said as they approached the car. "My truck should be ready in the next few days.

The gravel crunched underneath the men's feet as they approached the vehicle. Craig was slow to respond. Jeff stole a glance at the man to see if he had heard him. When Craig realized this, he gave a slight nod. "No problem."

As they opened the doors and climbed in, the passenger door squealed a bit, revealing its need for some

WD-40. The car's interior was clean despite its age. However, a green air freshener in the shape of a pine tree struggled to cover the smell of mud, sweat, and general funk that a construction worker left in it every day. The two men buckled their seatbelts and began the drive down the highway toward the interstate. After a minute, Jeff broke the silence.

"Jackson don't mean nothin' yelling at you. He's just a foreman being a foreman. He knows what you been through."

Craig took a deep breath and nodded. "I don't take it personal. Sometimes I just get caught up in my head and I need someone to help me get out."

He could tell that Jeff didn't know how to respond him sharing, and the silence from his coworker confirmed it. After the gray Camry got on the interstate, Jeff turned to look at Craig. "Beth wanted me to invite you for supper. She's cooked some spaghetti. Her grandma's Sicilian, so she makes homemade pasta. Not that dried-out box stuff. You ought to stay and eat with us."

Craig would have loved to, but he knew he couldn't. He didn't trust himself. It took all he had to get through the work day. "Can't tonight, but thanks for the invite."

The men looked out the window and made their way home with relatively little traffic for this time of day. The industrial area right before their exit was filled with warehouses, eight-story office buildings, and a large UPS hub. Convenience stores and fast-food restaurants were strategically located just off the interstate.

Jeff broke the silence. "It should be done when we get back. I'll get her to fix you a plate to take home."

"I don't want her to have to do that," Craig responded, but felt kind of excited about something homecooked for a change.

"Not taking no for an answer, especially since you won't let me give you any gas money. I'm telling you, you'll love it. You'll be ranting and raving about her cooking in the morning when you pick me up," Jeff declared.

Craig felt like it would be more of a hassle to argue with him, so he nodded his head in agreement. They took the next exit and drove past a Walmart and an old shopping mall. Then they turned into a subdivision filled with small brick homes, built in the '70s. Although the neighborhood had gone downhill a little in recent years, it was a great place to buy a starter home or to raise a family on a budget. Since Beth didn't work much and Craig knew Jeff wasn't making a lot of money, he figured their situation was the latter. They pulled into the driveway of a tan brick home with a freshly cut yard and yellow flowers in planters framing the front door.

"Give me just a minute," Jeff said as he climbed out of the vehicle. A black-haired girl, Jeff's daughter from a previous relationship, waved and smiled at Craig, who offered a weak smile and waved back. A few moments later, Jeff emerged, holding a bowl with a makeshift aluminum foil lid. Craig rolled down his window.

"Just bring me the bowl back tomorrow. She'll have both of our hides if you don't."

"Thanks," Craig replied. "Tell Beth I appreciate it."

Craig set the bowl on the passenger seat. As he began the three-mile stretch home, he could hear the old Johnny Cash song playing in his mind. He took a deep breath to try and regain his focus and was calmed by the smell of Italian food.

An empty bowl and three beer cans were all that remained of supper, and it had been significantly better than the bologna sandwich or fast-food burger he normally ate. He couldn't remember the last time he'd had a home-cooked meal. Something about it took him to a previous life. He recalled Tabatha's pot roast, and her banana pudding was the best he had ever eaten. He didn't want to let his thoughts go there. He knew what would happen; he'd wind up back at that dark place. He got up and washed the bowl, not wanting to forget it in the morning, and set it next to his car keys. Craig threw the beer cans away and then made his way to the living room. The tattered brown sectional overwhelmed the small room. He rested his legs on the 1980s coffee table he had picked up at a garage sale because Tabatha said no living room was complete without one. He adjusted his white T-shirt and orange pajama pants and grabbed the remote to turn on the television. Monday night football came on. He figured it was as good as anything else, so he leaned back and tried to get lost in the game.

Then it happened. It started with the song, Johnny Cash singing about Sunday morning again. He could see and smell the old bar; it was as real as anything that he'd ever experienced.

Why was he back here again? Why couldn't he just relax and watch the game? This made no sense. Did God hate him so much that he was destined to come back to this place over and over? The smell of fresh rain filled the night air. The dimly lit streets hid the storefronts. He thought about not walking into The Edge and instead going to any one of the nearby stores, or even running out into the hayfield. For some reason, however, he couldn't. Trying to go anywhere else never seemed to work. It was like his feet just wouldn't let him. He looked across the street into the dark fields, grasping for some idea, some hope, but nothing came to him.

Craig turned toward the neon lights flashing over the blacked-out windows and black door. The song continued to leak through the opening in the door and out into the parking lot. He could hear the tapping of his cowboy boots on the pavement as he walked toward the entrance; it reminded him of a beating heart.

As he approached the door, it opened. On instinct, he turned to the right and to the left but still couldn't discern who opened it. There was Kip behind the bar with a sly grin on his face, cleaning glasses. He spotted the couple in the back booth, hiding out; the man, as usual, was shooting Craig a dirty look. The old biker was trying to get his shot lined up while ignoring his back pain from repeatedly bending over the table. The jukebox was still lighting the hall to the bathrooms. The mechanic was nursing his cigarette, and the lady next to him was working her charm. Then, as always, was the long-haired fellow at the other end of the bar with a contented look about him, not really doing anything in particular, just kind of there.

For some reason, Craig was able to fight the urge to walk up to the bar for a brief moment. Instead, he stood and watched the guy. He was wearing a red T-shirt and a blue jeans. As the man shifted one of his hands, Craig noticed, even in the dim lighting of the bar, that he seemed to have something in his hand. No, it wasn't in his hand but *on* his hand, like a paint stain or tattoo.

"You coming to sit or what?" Kip hollered in a jovial manner.

Craig, confused by this change of events, nodded and made his way to the bar. "Whiskey," he replied, resuming the nightmarish script he thought he had to follow. The glass was set down in front of him, and Johnny Cash was singing about the agony of a Sunday morning.

Come on, Cash, why can't you sing anything else. Sing "Ring of Fire" or "A Boy Named Sue," but not this; for once, not this. Craig felt angry at the deceased singer for his melancholic musings. Then came the sound from his pocket. Reluctantly, he reached into his pocket to pull out the phone and heard a pounding.

Boom, Boom, Boom!

The sound scared the living daylights out of him, which was enough to transport him out of the bar and back to the couch. Then it happened again.

Boom, Boom, Boom!

It was a thud, a knocking, a rude call back to reality. Someone was at his door.

"Come on! Open up, Craig! You owe me."

Craig's heart pounded. He knew who it was. It was Anne, his landlord. It was the first day of the month, and if he didn't stop by her house with the rent check, she was going to come by and get it. As he struggled to get his heart rate back to normal, he thought of Tabatha's constant urging to quit renting and try to buy the old house, but it didn't make much sense to him now, other than not having to be scared to death by this lady on a monthly basis.

"I'm coming," he uttered as he got up, kicking the coffee table by accident. "Ow!"

"What did you say?" Anne asked through the door.

"I'm coming," he replied.

When Craig opened the door, he was greeted by the ridiculous print on Anne's sweatshirt: three cats playing with yarn in jewel tones. She adjusted her thick glasses, ran her hands through her curly brown hair, and walked into the house without an invite. "I'm sorry to scare you. I know you're good for the rent, but your memory these days is worse than my mother's, and I'm seventy!"

"It's okay," Craig said. "I was asleep. I'm sorry."

Craig made his way to the kitchen to grab his wallet, then pulled out a check and handed it to her.

"You said you were you asleep?" Anne's directness aggravated Craig. She took the check and put in in her oversized blue purse.

"Excuse me?"

"Were you really asleep? I know where you've been and what's happened, so I don't mind calling it like I see it."

"I don't understand," Craig responded.

"I'm about the only one you ever talk to, and I know what happened to Tabatha. I've seen that look in your eyes before, that zoning out. You sit out on that rocker in the front yard with a beer in your hand, looking like you've left the planet."

"Yeah, well, it's not like I want to go anywhere, but for some reason it just happens," Craig said as he scratched his greying beard, immediately regretting sharing so honestly.

"My niece."

"What?" Craig said, confused. "I'm sorry, Mrs. Anne, I didn't mean to bore you with my—"

She ignored his hesitation and continued. "My niece's oldest boy overdosed on that Fentanyl. She went and talked to this lady, a Christian counselor. Said it really helped. I got her to get me the card 'cause I thought I might go one of these days and talk about dealing with Ralph's death, but I think you need it more than me. I took a picture of it with my phone when she gave it to me because I'm old and lose stuff."

Craig remembered Anne's husband who had died early last year. He seemed like a kind man. A retired plant worker who had managed to buy a few rental properties to keep himself busy during his golden years. He did that for about a decade before the cancer got him. Craig wanted to tell Anne that he didn't want to talk to anyone and that his personal life was none of her business. However, it seemed easier to take the card and say thank you.

"Here it is," Anne said as she handed it to him.

"Thank you," he replied.

"I know what you're thinking." She put her hand on Craig's arm.

"What's that?"

"You're thinking you won't go."

"Counseling is not really my thing," Craig responded with sheepish smile. "I mean, if it works for someone else, that's great."

Anne waved her hand in the air, dismissing his statement. "If life stinks right now, I'm betting that sitting with someone for a few minutes won't make it stink any more. What if it made things just a little easier? You know Tabatha would want you to."

"Thank you," Craig said. "You have a good night."

Anne got the hint and made her way out as Craig walked back to the fridge.

ROCK BOTTOM

The night was a blur as usual. Craig laid down to sleep and forced his thoughts toward a pleasant night out that he and Tabatha had a couple of months before he lost her. He remembered telling her about how much his dad drank and that, somewhere along the way, he'd picked up the same habit. Tabatha was wearing a blue dress, something she had found on the clearance rack of Dillard's and bragged to her friends about. To most people, she was just a secretary at a middle school, but to Craig, she was the world. He had wasted his twenties and some of his thirties chasing women, drugs, alcohol, as well as fishing and hunting. Strange how life had taken all those things from him except the drinking. A bad drug trip that left him in the ER scared him too much to ever touch pills again. Fishing and hunting got too expensive, and hard living had left him overweight and less than appealing to most women.

He worked the oilfield for several years, then got laid off for drinking on the job and almost causing an accident. Word had spread to other companies in the area, and no one would hire him. However, a buddy managed to get him a construction job, and Craig figured out how to make his life more manageable, although the pay was less than what he was used to getting.

There was a pizza joint that he loved going to, and every Thursday night he'd go there and watch a game on the big-screen television. He enjoyed visiting with the waitresses and some of the regulars while drinking a few beers. That's where he met Tabatha. She was eating a salad at a table next to his, and they got to talking about life, family, past mistakes, and magically connected with each other. He thought she was beautiful. She was forty with silky blonde hair and had a positive outlook on life, despite some hard seasons she had endured. They hit it off and got married a few months after that.

"You gonna come to church with me?" Craig remembered Tabatha asking at the same pizza joint a year or so after they married. "That preacher and them people don't care about the stuff you say that keeps you from being able to go to church. Lots of them struggled with stuff in life too. Ain't no such thing as a perfect person."

While Craig was fascinated with the person of Jesus, even though he didn't know much about him, he hated the idea of organized religion. However, in that moment, he had to admit to himself that, once again, things were getting a little out of hand with his drinking, so maybe going to church wouldn't be such a bad thing.

"Maybe."

"Really?"

He nodded his head yes as he took a bite of his pizza. She continued to eat her salad with a smile on her face.

However, as much as he wanted to stay in that happy moment, he quickly moved from that memory back to The Edge, in what had to be a fever dream where over and over the same events played out time and time again. The song played on repeat in his mind, Johnny Cash once again talking about the two beers he drank for breakfast.

He could feel the eyes of Kip staring at him, the man in khakis giving him a dirty look, the smoke coming from the mechanic's cigarette, the woman laughing obnoxiously at a joke he believed was at his expense, and the unbothered man at the end of the bar with long hair and dark skin, no drink in his hand, who appeared so out of place that it annoyed Craig.

Several hours later, the beeping of the alarm went off, and Craig woke up feeling like he hadn't slept at all, wanting a drink with every fiber of his being. Against his better judgement, he gave into that desire and poured some whiskey into the coffee in his thermos. He hurriedly got dressed, threw on his construction vest, made sure he had his hard hat, grabbed his keys, and ran out the door. He was halfway to work when he realized he'd forgotten to pick up Jeff. The morning traffic had him running behind schedule, but not knowing what else to do, he took the nearest exit and approached the ramp to get on the interstate in the other direction. The clock on the dash made him nervous, so he picked up his speed and weaved back and forth between lanes. When he exited the interstate and finally turned onto Jeff's road, he sped past a stopped school bus. And then, right on cue, the blue lights and police siren activated.

"You've got to be kidding me!" Craig said as he looked in the rearview. He pulled over to the shoulder and grabbed his license and registration. Then he thought about the whiskey in his coffee and squeezed his eyes shut. He grabbed a stick of cinnamon gum that he always kept in the console, unwrapped it, and popped in his mouth, hoping for the best. A wave of nervousness swept over him. It had been years since he had been pulled over, but there was a point where he had nearly lost his license, and the fear of that was now weighing heavy on him.

A tap on the window pulled him back to reality. A young police officer with a goatee had his hands on the top of his black vest. Craig rolled the window down and rested his hands on the steering wheel, his license and registration at the ready.

"Mr. Mario Andretti. I guess you know why I pulled you over," the officer said in a serious tone, despite his attempt at a joke.

"Yes, sir," Craig replied with as much sincerity as he could muster. "I'm sorry. I'm running late and was trying to pick up a coworker who needed a ride. I wasn't paying attention. I have no excuse."

"License and registration, please," the officer said stoically, not revealing his intentions to Craig.

Craig handed the papers to the officer, who returned to the police car. Craig sat there and waited for what seemed to be an eternity, and carelessly picked up his thermos and took a large swig, only realizing what he had done after he set it down. "I'm such an idiot."

He closed his eyes and tried to calm himself down, only to find himself back on the dimly lit street, the faint melody of the Johnny Cash song playing again.

Not now, Craig thought to himself. However, against his own wishes, he walked to the door with the neon sign shining over it. Light from the bar poured through the crack in the door, and the song's volume rose with each step. He forced himself to stop for a minute and look around. He fought the desire to go inside; he felt the pull from deep within. He stared at the black door and the strip of light along the edges while Johnny Cash went on about wanting a drink. It was as if he were approaching a portal to another world. He took a few steps closer and focused on the paint, which hid numerous cracks and splinters. Then, as he looked at the knob, something startled him.

Tap. Tap. Tap.

This was new; Craig wasn't sure what was happening.

Tap. Tap. Tap.

The tapping became louder.

"Sir, I need you to roll your window back down." The officer's voice pulled Craig back to reality.

He frantically rolled the window down and apologized to the officer.

"You okay, Mr. Brown?" the officer asked.

Craig nodded his head as he looked the officer in the eyes. "I'm fine. Sorry, just a little tired."

"Haven't had anything to drink this morning, have you?" he asked flippantly.

The question brought Craig's fears back to the surface. Was this it? Was he busted? "No, sir. Just coffee," he replied as he pointed at the thermos, hoping the officer didn't want to inspect it.

He hesitated for several seconds as he looked at Craig, then he looked up at traffic passing by and back down at Craig. "Look, I'm not supposed to do this. Passing like you did is a big deal, but I've been late to work before and made dumb decisions. Let's just do better. Can we do that?"

"Absolutely, Officer," Craig said with gratitude in his voice. "It won't happen again."

The policeman nodded and headed back to his vehicle. Craig started his car and drove toward his coworker's house. Jeff was sitting in a chair on the lawn with his work gear. As soon as Craig pulled up, he hurried to the vehicle, and the two men headed to work.

"Brown! My office, now!" the foreman hollered to Craig as soon as he and Jeff walked onto the site.

"Sorry, man," Jeff said as he walked toward the work crew.

"No worries," Craig replied, but he didn't believe it. He could feel his stomach churning as he approached the tan trailer that served as the office. Jackson, the foreman, had already entered the trailer and closed the white metal door behind him. Craig turned the knob and walked onto the faded, mock-wood laminate flooring. Wood paneling lined the walls, with only a few legally required posters displaying workers' rights hanging on the walls. In the center was a gray card table and a few folding chairs around it.

"Sit, please," Jackson instructed.

"Yes, sir," Craig replied. "Sorry, Mr. Jackson. I got off to a bad start this morning and forgot I had to pick up Jeff. It won't happen again."

Jackson was probably thirty-five, and his black hair went down to his shoulders, which were quite broad. He wore a red polo with a yellow vest over it; his hard hat was set down on the table next to him. He had a perpetual grumpy look when he walked the site, but was generally a courteous man, and most of the men had no issues with him. Craig knew that everything was entirely his fault. He had no one to blame but himself, just like all his other mistakes.

"You sure about that?" Jackson pressed as he leaned in a little.

"Yes, sir. I am."

"Look, I'll be one hundred percent honest with you. If it wasn't that Jeff needed you for a ride, and that he's one of the best workers on the site, I'd have been real tempted to let you go this morning." Jackson looked Craig directly in the eyes. He didn't know what to say, so he kept silent and took the scolding as best he could, knowing that he deserved it. "You come in here late about once a week, and a time or two I swore I smelled liquor on you. Sometimes you'll just zone out on me! I got sympathy for you. I really do. I know you've been through some stuff, and I really hate that for you. But listen to me and listen good. That sympathy only goes so far. I got deadlines and safety requirements, so you need to get yourself together. If you're looking for help, the company offers all sorts of help for whatever you're facing. Becky in HR can get you set up with a counselor or in a program or whatever. But you've got to do it. You must take the step. No one else is gonna do it for you. And if you can't get yourself together, next time we're sitting in here it won't be nearly as pleasant of a meeting."

"I understand," Craig replied. Then he looked down nervously at the gray table, waiting to be dismissed.

Jackson slid a clipboard over to him; it was a report form stating that he had been formally warned of an issue and this was the second occurrence of such an event. And as a result of this meeting, Craig was to be more focused on his job and to arrive on time. Looking over it made Craig feel like a child. He knew he was supposed to sign it, so he grabbed a pen and hurriedly scribbled his name and the date.

"Get it together. I don't want to lose you," Jackson warned.

Craig nodded his head and made his way outside.

HUNGOVER

Craig went to the pizza joint, the one where he'd met Tabatha. While he waited for his meal, he nursed a beer and played with a business card taken from his pocket. He drummed it up against the table, rubbed the embossed words, and then stared at it. In that moment, he couldn't hear the television playing highlights of yesterday's game or the group of college students sitting at the bar laughing. His mind was only on this card and what he was supposed to do with it. He had spent most of his life not letting people in. Sure, he used to love a good party; sure, he knew how to have a good time with a beautiful woman. But those things didn't really allow someone know him. Craig had received a masterclass in being distant by watching his dad. The only person growing up who he felt close to was his mom, but she died unexpectedly during Craig's junior year of high school. Her death only heightened the strain he felt with his father. Tabatha had been one of the few whom he'd opened up to, and even then it was a struggle.

He stared at the business card intently. It was white with blue trim. The small logo depicted one hand reaching out for another, and the raised lettering read, "Dr. Lisa Thrum: Certified Christian Counselor." The numbers on the bottom of the page invited him to call. He figured it would be too late. It was already 6:30 p.m. But as thought about his run-in with the police that morning and nearly losing his job, he knew he needed to do something. His hand went to grab the phone in his pocket.

Why was this so hard? At the end of the day, talking to a stranger who was paid to keep his secrets wasn't really that big of a deal; yet in his mind, he could hear long-gone friends chuckling at him.

"Here's your pizza," the waitress said as she set down a medium-size pizza. The smell of meats and vegetables sinking into the piping hot cheese and sauce was enough to grab his attention for a moment. He tucked the card back into his pocket and let one of his favorite meals relieve the stresses of a rough day.

Craig remembered getting to work the next day and congregating for a group meeting with the crew. What he didn't remember was drifting off. He found himself back there again; the coolness and dampness of the night sent a chill down his spine. The darkness around him felt even heavier than it normally did. The Cash song played softly, and the light from behind the door beckoned him. This time, there was no resistance. He just walked toward the door until it opened. The man in the corner table with the "other" woman shot him a dirty look. He turned his eyes toward the old biker playing pool alone, fighting through his aches and pains. His gaze moved past the hallway lit by the jukebox to the mechanic smoking next to the woman laughing. Kip, the barkeep, was cleaning glasses but managed to look up at Craig and smile a little.

Then, at the far end of the bar, the long-haired man with the dark complexion just sat there, not drinking or talking with anyone. Craig kept his eyes on him until the man turned and smiled. In some strange way, that smile gave him the only peace he could ever find in this strange place. Then, as if on cue, Craig made his way to a stool at the bar and waited for Kip to look at him. Craig nodded his head, and Kip poured some whiskey into a glass and set it down by Craig's hand. The smell rose to Craig's nose, and he wasn't sure if he hated it or loved it. Regardless, he quickly drank it and watched Kip clean glasses while he waited for his phone to ring.

Initially, he told himself that he didn't care. It didn't matter if he answered the call or not; none of this was real. However, despite what he told himself, dread still weighed heavy on him. Kip gave him a look that conveyed pity; it felt appropriate. Then, instead of the phone ringing like he anticipated, an unexpected voice startled him.

"Come on, Craig. Snap out of it," he heard Jeff whisper and felt his shoulder being shaken. There he was, with his coworkers, standing in a circle. One of the younger men there was shooting him a perplexed glance; however, it didn't seem like anyone else had noticed, including the foreman. In fact, it seemed Jackson hadn't missed a beat in explaining a new safety protocol they were required to follow. Once he finished his explanation, everyone was sent home a few minutes early.

"Thanks for snapping me out of it," Craig said to Jeff.

"Why do you do that? What's going on in your head?" Jeff asked.

"You don't want to know."

They approached the vehicle, and Craig started the car and blasted the air conditioning. They sat in silence for a moment as they began the ride home until Craig finally broke the silence. "Sorry, I forgot the bowl again. I'm gonna grab it and bring over after I drop you off."

"No problem. Want to stay for supper when you drop it off? I think she's cooking lasagna," Jeff replied.

"Can't tonight," Craig responded with a bit of determination in his voice. "I need to make a phone call."

The phone rang twice, and since it was already after five, Craig expected the voicemail to pick up; however, a woman's voice answered, and it caught him off guard.

"This is Dr. Lisa Thrum, how can I help you?"

"Um, yes, my name's Craig Brown, and I was . . ." Craig couldn't make out the proper words and seriously considered hanging up. Then he tried again. "Someone gave me your number and I, well—"

Sensing his struggle, Dr. Thrum spoke in a firm but gentle voice. "Mr. Brown, would you like to schedule an appointment to come and visit with me? Is that why you're calling?"

"Yeah, yeah. I guess I've come to a point where talking with someone could be helpful. I'm kind of stuck in this thing."

"Lots of my clients work during the day, so a couple days a week I work from noon to eight. Tomorrow is one of those nights, and I just had a client cancel his appointment for tomorrow evening. Would you like to come in at six tomorrow night?"

Craig was taken aback by how quickly this whole thing was getting started. "Uh, yeah, yeah. I think I'm free tomorrow night."

"Great. Bring your insurance card with you if you have one. If not, we will figure out the best payment option for you."

"Will do."

"Craig, one more thing. Take a deep breath. It's going to be okay. I'm looking forward to working with you."

He had driven by the building where Dr. Thrum's office was located hundreds of times. It was only a few miles from his own house. The ten-story building was the result of a rapid expansion of this part of town back in the late '90s. The building still felt modern. The sound of a large water fountain greeted Craig as he entered the building; the smell of a small coffee cart by the entrance made him crave a cup. However, the lady who worked it was closing down for the day. A few businessmen were visiting as they walked toward the exit. He nodded at them and made his way to a directory on the wall. A quick glance showed that Dr. Thrum's office was on the fourth floor, Suite 12.

A short elevator ride later, the metallic doors opened to reveal a black-tiled hallway with a few ornamental plants strategically placed. From a window, Craig could see the lights from a nearby shopping center as dusk was starting to fall over the city. Suite 12 was at the end of the hallway. It was a short walk, but for Craig it felt like one of the longest he had ever taken. His whole life, he had strived to bottle everything up and find a way to push through and deal with whatever came his way. However, going into that office and having a conversation with this counselor meant admitting that everything was not okay and, in fact, he needed help. While part of him was not ready to admit this, another part of him didn't feel like he had any other option. These trips to The Edge were ruining his life. If he lost his job, he didn't know what he'd do.

He walked to the door and read the plaque: "Suite #12: Dr. Lisa Thrum, Christian Counselor." Part of him expected the door to open like the at The Edge, but it didn't. He'd have to open this one himself. When he turned the lever and pushed on it, the door didn't budge. It was heavy, but he was strong enough that he shouldn't have any issues opening it. Maybe it was locked. Was this a sign to go back home? However, as he pushed firmly up on the door lever, it finally opened without much effort. Inside was a small waiting room. His eyes went to an end table topped with several magazines, and a small bookshelf in the corner featuring a variety of different pamphlets. Cushioned flower-print chairs lined the wall, and a receptionist sat behind a glass screen next to another wooden door.

The receptionist looked to be in her twenties and smiled as Craig walked in.

"Hello, how are you today?" she asked with just the right amount of perkiness, which helped Craig feel a little more at ease. "Sorry about that door. Maintenance needs to come and work on it."

Craig walked over to the window and gave her a small smile. "I'm okay," he said hesitantly. "I'm Craig Brown, and I have an appointment with Dr. Thrum."

"Yes, sir," she replied and handed him a clipboard. "If you can fill this out, I'll let Dr. Lisa know you're here."

A few minutes later, after Craig had returned the paperwork, a sharply dressed woman in her late forties opened the door.

"Hello, Mr. Brown. I'm Dr. Lisa Thrum. Call me Dr. Lisa." She gave him a warm smile. "You can follow me to my office."

Craig nodded his head but felt too uneasy to speak. He followed her down a carpeted hallway to a large office with bookshelves packed with books covering three walls, a small desk in one corner, and a few chairs on the other side of the room. She motioned toward a chair and sat down across from him. Craig sat down and nervously fidgeted with his pockets, waiting for a few seconds for Dr. Lisa to start things off.

"Tell me about yourself, Craig," she began.

"Me, well . . . uh," Craig replied, once again struggling to get his words together. "I'm sorry. This sure is tough. I'm not really a 'talk to people about myself' kind of guy."

"That's okay, we don't need to dive deep into anything yet. Let's get to know each other a bit first."

Craig nodded and let out a small sigh of relief, then only partly listened to the doctor sharing about her garden and her two dogs, as well as a little about the church she attended. Nothing over the top, just surface-level stuff. Craig followed suit and talked about the community he grew up in, the kind of work he did, and what sports teams he liked. While Craig still didn't consider himself to be very good at this type of conversation as opposed to Tabatha and some of his coworkers, the conversation was not entirely unpleasant. However, after fifteen minutes, it became clear that the small-talk portion was nearing its end.

"So, what brings you here to me, Mr. Brown? What do you really want to talk about?"

He took a deep breath and stated what he had practiced saying in his mind a few times on his way over here. "About a year ago, my wife died. We were staying at my sister-in-law's. There was a program at her church that my wife, Tabatha, wanted us all to go to. Instead, I went to this run-down bar. At this point, I'm not sure what I really remember from the night or what actually happened. It's hard to explain. In some ways everything kind of blurs together, but in other ways it's all very clear. So like I said, I went to this seedy bar. The kind of place you only go to when you're desperate to get a drink, which was where I was, in a town I wasn't very familiar with, needing a drink. Anyway, the bartender's name was Kip. Don't ask me why this stood out, but it did. Then I remember getting the phone call that my wife and sister-in-law had been in a car accident, and my wife had died."

Craig looked at Dr. Lisa, who seemed to be listening attentively but was not eager to speak when he paused. After a few more seconds of silence, he continued. "My problem is that I keep finding myself back in that bar; not physically, but in my mind. But it seems as real as if I were there; it feels as real as this conversation we are having right now. But when I go there, other than the bartender, I'm not sure if any of those people were actually there or not that night. I go in, see these same people every time, then I go and sit at the bar and order some whiskey. After I drink it, the cell phone in my pocket rings, and I get the news that my wife has died. Sometimes this happens five or six times during the day. It happens every night when I go to bed, usually multiple times. It's interfering with my job. I often lose focus and mentally check out of the real world. That's why I'm here. I don't know how to make it stop."

"Let me first say that I'm sorry for your loss and everything that you've been going through. I know that must be very hard," Dr. Lisa responded. "This may seem like a stupid question, so forgive me, but do you have any idea as to why this might be happening?"

"I don't know . . . guilt, maybe," Craig replied as he looked down at the floor and tried not to show any emotion. "I had been telling Tabatha that I was planning on going to church and making some changes to try to get my drinking under control, but I kept putting it off. I think that night, if I had gone, I would have driven the car because I usually did when we were all together. If I had, then there might not have been an accident."

"What did grieving look like for you?"

"I don't know. I'm not really an emotional guy, but it was the hardest thing I've ever experienced. I tried to keep it all together. I'm pretty good around people. I can usually keep it together. But I really struggle when I'm by myself. Drinking helps, even though I know it shouldn't. I don't want it to."

"Craig, do you believe in God or a higher power?"

"I've always been interested in Jesus. I've had a draw to Him, but I've always kept myself from thinking about it too much. I figure I'm not the kind of guy someone like Jesus would help out."

"Why would you say that? I'm a Christian, and I've seen Jesus help a lot of people. Some of them are murderers serving time in prison; some are adulterers and addicts. I'm not saying they didn't have to do their time or deal with the consequences of their actions, but they found peace in Jesus." Dr. Lisa offered these words to Craig in a no-pressure way that seemed to make him reflect on these truths.

He sat in silence for a moment, then shook his head, dismissing this notion of peace in Jesus being available to him. "I need to know how to stop these visions, thoughts, or whatever is happening to me. This is my problem. I'm not really looking for religion, no offense, so why does that matter?"

The doctor seemed unphased by Craig's counter. "When I see someone experiencing something like this, my first thought is that your brain is trying to process something. If it were happening to me, I would pray and ask for insight from God to understand why this is happening. If you're not a person of faith, I would try to figure out if there's some meaning here. What you experienced was a traumatic event. Our brains do weird things with trauma because we don't know what to do with it. So, my first guidance would be to try and see if there's any meaning hidden in all of this. Maybe your brain is trying to put something together and it doesn't know how to, so you need to play detective."

"How?" Craig asked with eyes raised in keen interest.

"Well, we can talk through what you're seeing, as much as you're comfortable telling me. Then there's something else you can try, even though it may seem a bit odd."

"Odd? What do you mean?"

"Have you ever heard of lucid dreaming?"

"No, I don't think so."

Dr. Lisa sat back in her chair and looked up for a few seconds. "How do I explain this? Well, it's when you're in a dream state, yet you have control of what you do in the dream to some extent. Sometimes when people mentally revisit traumatic events, they can gain some sort of control over them. Have you ever tried this?"

Craig nodded. "A little. I've had a few limited instances of control, but most of it feels like a script that plays out involuntarily, so it's hard to do anything different."

"Next time you find yourself visiting this bar, try everything in your power to not follow the script. Tell me what you see, if you're okay with that."

Craig took a deep breath and then described every detail that he could recall, from the water puddle in the parking lot, to the sign over the door, to how the door opened on its own, to the song playing, to the couple at the corner booth, to the old biker, to the jukebox lighting the hallway to the bathrooms, to the couple at one end of the bar, to Kip the bartender, and finally, to the smiling man with the dark complexion and the long hair at the other end of the bar. Then he told of his whiskey order, the dread in those final moments, and the phone call that ended everything.

She took a minute to process the scene, then finally spoke. "I don't have any magical answers. I think next time you find yourself there, run around the parking lot, throw your phone in the water puddle, go mess with the cheating couple, talk to the biker, change the song on the jukebox, ask the lady what the mechanic said that was so funny, tell Kip a joke and see if he laughs, and introduce yourself to the long-haired guy sitting alone. Just do something. Stir things up a bit, and see if your brain doesn't reveal something else to you that can help you make sense of what you're supposed to be figuring out so you can move on with your life."

"That's it?" Craig asked, not angry but perplexed at what the proposed solution was.

"For right now, I think it may be a good place to start. Make notes in a journal of anything that you do different or that changes. Then let's get together soon, maybe another evening appointment, and see where we are then," Dr. Lisa offered. "I'm a Christian and a Christian counselor, and I believe firmly in prayer. Can I pray with you about this?"

Craig nodded his head, mostly out of a desire to be polite. When she bowed her head and closed her eyes, he followed suit. "God, I pray that you would help Craig understand what it is that is going on in his mind. Show your Son Jesus to him and the great love that you have for him. Help him as he begins to work through this. Amen."

Craig thanked her and then Dr. Lisa walked him out. The receptionist helped him set up his next appointment. He then made his way downstairs and headed back home with just the slightest bit of hope that he could figure out what was at the root of all of this and finally put an end to it.

CHANGING THE ORDER

There he was, back in the parking lot. Even though he knew he was home in his bed, he was also here, in this place. It was the song that gave it away. Johnny Cash crooning about not being able to find a way to hold his head that didn't hurt.

This was it. Craig took a deep breath and told himself to pay attention and to not be afraid to try different things. Remembering the comment about throwing the phone in the water puddle, he thought to himself that this seemed as good of an idea as any. However, there was some force that didn't want to let him change the script. It was hard to describe, but it felt strong.

"You're in charge, Craig. This is your world," he told himself.

Something about the reminder made him feel stronger, like he was up for the task. He put his hand in his pocket, picked up the phone, and walked to the water puddle in the dark parking lot. The lights from the sign above the door reflected dimly in the water. He dropped the phone to the ground and watched as it crashed into the water and broke the reflection of the neon lights. Craig then made his way to the door as the song continued. He knew what he was going to do next.

As the door opened on its own, he walked all the way to the back, past the man in khakis giving Craig harsh looks. He walked past the tables. The old biker shooting pool gave a slight head nod to Craig, and Craig returned the gesture. The orange and green lights from the jukebox shined all around Craig, and he looked at the display and saw the title: "Sunday Morning Coming Down." He noticed there were credits in the machine. He pressed the button to end the current option and typed in the first alternate option he saw. A36 and "Always on My Mind" by Willie Nelson began to play. He took a deep breath, overwhelmed with the joy of not having to hear another stanza of the song that had been haunting him for so long.

Craig made his way over to the man in the khakis and a dress shirt. The man's initial response was, as expected, to look at Craig nervously. However, the closer Craig got, the more the man's facial expressions scrunched with anger and widened with fear and discomfort. The woman next to him in the green dress looked at the man next to her in hopes of getting some kind of clue as to how to react. By the time Craig arrived at the table, she was sitting up straight and looking in Craig's direction but not in the eyes.

"Good evening," Craig said.

"Can we help you?" the man replied sternly enough to convey that helping was the last thing on his mind.

"I sure hope so," Craig said with a slight chuckle. "Can you guys tell me what you're doing here?"

"Just trying to get a drink and have a few minutes together," the man responded. "A little alone time." There was an emphasis in his voice on the word "alone."

Craig understood the hint but wasn't willing to give up yet. "Why here?"

The woman in the green dress finally spoke. "Because we like being here, in the corner, in the dark, doing what we enjoy without anyone giving us much attention. This is our life. We're trying to figure out what makes us happy."

For the first time since he had returned and began practicing what Dr. Lisa had recommended, Craig felt like he was making some progress, like something was being uncovered. As he looked over the couple, he noticed the man's hands resting on the table; there was an indentation on his ring finger where it was clear that a ring had been worn, even if one wasn't on the finger now.

"You guys married?" Craig asked.

The man crossed his arms in an attempt to conceal his empty ring finger. "What's it to you? Why do you care?"

"I lived like you for a long time. Nothing but heartache, chasing one thing after another, not paying any mind to what's around you. If you've got a good wife at home, you ought to put this aside and go home to her." Then he turned his eyes to the woman. "Ma'am, I don't know what you really expect to get out of this other than a few fun nights, but there's nothing worthwhile at the end of this road. You guys don't need to be here. This place is a dump." Out of the corner of his eye he could see Kip shooting him a dirty look after overhearing his comment. Seeing the bartender worked up was both unexpected and interesting.

Craig was impressed by his charge to the couple, then he remembered that they weren't real. All it made him do was reflect on a life of one-night stands and regret from not treating women better—also, not treating himself better. It wasn't until he met Tabatha that he believed he could be the settling down type who was worthy of love. As he walked away from the table, he overheard the man and the woman in discussion, but not of the pleasant kind. Kip motioned for him to come to the bar. This caught Craig off guard, so he made his way over and sat down.

"You like running off my customers?" Kip asked in a deep, gruffy voice as he placed a glass under the counter.

Craig turned around and watched the man in khaki pants and the woman in the green dress leave the bar. Then he turned back to Kip. "Sorry, my friend, but they didn't need to be here anyway."

"Hmm," Kip said before grabbing something under the counter. Craig assumed it was a glass, but he set down the old cell phone Craig had thrown into the puddle and looked at him straight in the eyes. "I think this is yours."

The phone then vibrated and rang. Craig looked at it, filled at first with dread, as if he was losing control again. However, as he tried to get his bearings, he looked confidently at Kip. "I don't think so."

"I think you're lying. You need to answer it," Kip urged.

Craig hesitated, not sure of what to do. The two men looked at each other as if it were some game of chicken, one waiting for the other to break away first. After several seconds, Craig grabbed the phone and threw it toward the shelf lined bottles behind the bar. A few bottles fell to the ground. One shattered, letting liquor flow down freely. Then something else happened.

Boom.

Everything shook, and Craig woke up in his room to hear a downpour outside his house. He looked at the clock. It was five a.m. His cell phone was next to the clock, and across the display was a text: "Work cancelled for the day."

The news was a surprise. Craig realized that he probably should have paid more attention to the weather. In his younger days, he would have loved the time off from work, but now it just served as a temptation to drink, get lost in his thoughts, and keep him from the little bit of remaining human contact that he allowed himself. However, today was different. He'd been given a homework assignment, and he thought this might be the perfect opportunity to work on it. He got out of bed, threw on some shorts and a T-shirt, brushed his teeth, got a cup of coffee, and sat down in his chair in the living room with an old notepad. He made a few notes about what had changed when he decided to talk to the couple. For the first time in a long time, he could feel a bit of hope and accomplishment. Perhaps he'd be able to get to the bottom of what his brain (or soul) was trying to tell him.

After writing down a few notes, he set the notepad down, took the last swig from his coffee cup, and set it on the coffee table next to the notepad. Craig leaned back, closed his eyes, and listened to the pitter patter of the rain. He expected it to lull him back to dreams of the bar, a chance to engage with those there; however, for the first time in a long time, he fell into a deep and dreamless sleep.

Craig woke up and could tell by the rhythm of the rain hitting the roof that it was slacking up and wouldn't last much longer. A quick glance at the clock on the wall revealed that he had been asleep for a few hours. He wondered if the clock was wrong. He hadn't slept so deeply in a long time. The odd thing was that for the first time that he could remember, he wouldn't have minded zoning out to The Edge. Ordinarily, he would have gone there multiple times while he slept or laid in bed, but not today. Something about it made him wonder whether he should be upset or happy. However, instead of debating the issue, he got up, fixed himself a bowl of cereal, then turned on the television. Nothing was on this time of day but court shows, talk shows, reruns, and game shows. Craig settled on a rerun of an old '90s sitcom, one that Tabatha used to watch. He never could understand its appeal, but she sure loved it. She'd laugh her head off at some of the cheesy jokes and it would almost annoy Craig, like it was something he wasn't smart enough to understand.

"This is so stupid!" he said out loud.

After finishing his cereal, he set the bowl on the coffee table next to the notepad. He grabbed the notepad and added a line about not being able to go back to The Edge and falling into a much deeper sleep the previous evening than he had in a long time. Then he set it back down and stared brainlessly at the television, not really thinking about anything, just letting it all wash over him. In the midst of zoning out, he found himself back in the old familiar parking lot, greeted by the voice of Johnny Cash singing about Sunday morning again.

"I thought I had changed the song," Craig said. Then he wondered if everything reset when he left, and if it did, what was he supposed to do now? Aggravated but not yet defeated, he reached into his pocket and pulled out his phone. He turned toward the field across the street from the bar and threw it as far as he could, hoping some cow would step on it. Then he turned and made his way into the bar; the door, as expected, opened as he approached it. He looked around the bar and saw the same familiar cast of characters. Kip was washing a glass, the man with the long hair and dark complexion was sitting by himself; at the other end of the bar was the mechanic smoking a cigarette and the woman next to him, laughing obnoxiously at his jokes. The jukebox looked the same. The old biker played pool, and the couple in the booth… Wait a second! The booth was empty. He did a double take to make sure he hadn't looked at the wrong booth, then looked all throughout the large bar. They weren't there! The song had returned, but not the couple. Craig had managed to change something. This felt promising. He walked to the juke box and put on an Allen Jackson song, then walked over to the old biker.

"You winning?" Craig asked the man who was studying the table for his next shot.

"I don't think my back is. My body hates me bending over like this, but my mind is convinced that it loves to play, so every now and then I come here and give in a bit. I always wind up regretting it though." The old biker took his shot with confidence and watched as the cue ball knocked the two-ball into a corner pocket.

"Impressive shot," Craig said as he watched the man rub his lower back.

"Thanks. If you think that's good, you should have seen me when I could really play."

"You from here?" Craig asked, wanting to know a little more about the man's story and if there was something he was supposed to learn.

"No, not really. This is just where I wound up," the old biker replied before lining up to take another shot. Craig gave him his space, and after several seconds of positioning and concentration, another successful shot was made.

"What do you mean?"

The biker looked annoyed for a second that someone had interrupted his game, but Craig watched as something shifted in the man's mind, and he decided to lay the pool stick down on the table. "Home sucked, so I joined up with some guys and rode wherever the wind would take us. Somewhere along the way, they all settled down and moved on with life. I guess I forgot to do that. I might have stopped if somewhere ever felt like home, but no place ever did. I didn't really mean to stop here. I've told myself that one of these days I'll get back on the road, but I think that life might have left me while I was here."

"What keeps this town from being home?"

"You sound like old Jay at the bar over there," the biker replied with a chuckle, pointing his pool stick to the man with the long hair at the bar. "He keeps telling me that I need to go hang out with him, and I keep telling him I can't yet, got too much going on. I think he knows I'm lying."

This made Craig curious. The biker's statements made him wonder about Jay's story? He seemed different than everyone else here, like he didn't have the weight on him that Craig felt the others had. "What have you got to lose? Why not see what he's talking about?"

The old biker leaned up against the table and rubbed his neck for a moment, then looked intently at Craig. "We tend to settle into what we believe about ourselves and about life, and it's hard to get out of those places. Then by the time we think we really ought to, it's like something in us just can't let go. I guess I could ask you the same question: Why do you keep coming here? You know you shouldn't be here, yet here you are."

The question perplexed Craig; it got to the core of everything. He was stuck in his beliefs about his own failures, that he wasn't worth cleaning up, that he belonged here in some messed-up way.

"Just leave and don't come back," the old biker said. "Why not?"

Craig knew that this was intended as a challenge to prove a point, but it certainly got his mind working. He had flipped the script once already. Why not again? "Let's go. Let's leave and get some fresh air."

The biker smiled. His long gray beard lifted up a little with the grin.

"Come on! Let's go," Craig urged with a motion to the door. Kip set a glass down on the bar so hard the clank of it was heard throughout the bar, even getting the mechanic and the women next to him to turn their heads. It sent a chill down Craig's back, unsettling him. He couldn't understand the barkeeper's aggression. The biker turned his eyes to the bar, almost as if looking for some approval from Kip.

"Don't rush off, boys. Free round on me," Kip offered with a menacing smile.

The old man turned to Craig, the lines in his cheeks and forehead becoming more defined by the angle of light shining on him. "I think I'm good. I'd like some fresh air."

Craig smiled as he made his way to the door. The older man walked slowly but confidently behind him. Craig had to push the door open. It was heavier than he expected. Once opened, the old biker walked out, and Craig let the door shut behind them. He paused to visit with the old biker, but he had already turned back toward town and was walking away.

"Where are you heading?" Craig called out.

Without turning around, the old biker replied, "I think I'll head to Jay's place. Maybe it'll feel like home."

Craig watched him go down the road. In the distance, he could have sworn he heard his phone ringing from the field. He didn't care though. His mind was racing about his encounter with the biker. The next thing he knew, he was back on his couch. The rain had stopped, and the sun was shining through the living room window.

RETURNING BLOWS

Two more days passed without any further trips to the bar. In some ways, Craig felt relieved, like he was getting a piece of his life back. He felt more effective at work and had no more issues with his foreman. He even went to dinner with Jeff and his wife Friday night. Craig listened to their daughter's knock-knock jokes and even contributed a few of his own. When he went to bed, he slept almost as soon as his head hit the pillow, no restless dreaming.

Another strange thing was happening. This whole process of figuring out what his mind was telling him made him detest the alcohol that he had consumed every day, so he quit drinking. However, that choice did lead to some nausea, headaches, and nervousness. While it wasn't severe, his body was definitely letting him know that it wasn't happy about his decision. Still, there was something occurring inside of him that made him want to dig deep into the recent happenings with as clear a mind as possible. Part of him felt like God and Tabatha were speaking to him in some special way, and he didn't want to miss what was being said.

With nearly three days of no trips to The Edge, he began to feel that perhaps he had conquered this struggle and could move on with his life. Part of him even thought about calling Dr. Lisa and telling her that he wasn't feeling a need to come back in. Then something happened in the most unusual place. Saturday morning Jeff called and asked Craig to bring him to the mechanic because his vehicle was ready. Craig agreed and drove him to the shop. He decided to pick up a sausage biscuit on his way home, and as he waited in line he suddenly heard the Johnny Cash song he dreaded so much. Part of him was disappointed that he was being blindsided like this. He really felt like he had been making progress, but there was the song, blaring out, with no way to turn the volume down. In frustration, Craig shook his head to get it out of his mind and then opened his eyes to find himself standing right outside of the familiar bar. It was powerful and real, but so was the realization that he was in a drive-through and needed to regain his focus as soon as possible.

Without much thought, he found himself talking out loud in a panicked way. "Come on, Craig, get it together. You can't do this right now!" He closed his eyes and opened them again, hoping to be back in his vehicle. It didn't work. Craig then fell to his knees in the parking lot and could feel the rough gravel cutting into his knees. He slammed his fists on the ground and then became interrupted by the sound of his own car horn. Suddenly, he was back in his vehicle and realized that he wasn't pounding the ground with his fists but his steering well, and in the process had activated his vehicle's horn. The man in front of him stuck his hand out of the window and shook his fist at Craig.

Craig rolled down his window and yelled, "I'm sorry! It was an accident." The man didn't respond. Craig could feel the blood rushing to his face, and for the first time in a few days, he thought about getting a drink to take the edge off. Then the thought occurred to him that maybe he had to go back to The Edge. Maybe he was supposed to dive a little deeper into the world his mind had created and figure out what he needed to do to make these visions stop once and for all.

Two hours later, Craig sat in his backyard listening to neighborhood kids playing in their above-ground pool. Behind the fence on the other side of the yard, he could hear Mr. Jones weed-eating, the smooth humming sound interrupted occasionally by the crackling of the weed-eater getting too close to the fence or a potted plant. He had been unsuccessful in returning to The Edge but had managed to relax and even doze off a time or two. He contemplated cutting his own grass when he heard a yell from the front yard.

"You back there, Craig?" Anne yelled.

"Yes, ma'am," he replied. He got up and opened the fence door to let her into the backyard without going through the house. "What brings you over?" He smiled at her brightly colored Hawaiian shirt and white shorts. He couldn't tell what was whiter, her shorts or her legs.

"Now don't you laugh at me, Craig Brown. I'm trying to get some sunshine on these old legs," she said with a smirk.

"No, ma'am, I wouldn't dare," he replied, holding back a chuckle. "Take a seat." He motioned toward an empty lawn chair.

"No, not today," Anne said. "I just had you on my mind today. I was running some errands and wanted to come by."

He offered her a smile, and the two stood there in the silence for several seconds before she broke it. "But you look good today. Better than last time I saw you, like you're carrying a little less weight."

"Thank you. I think I'm feeling a little better these last few days."

"It's going to be all right, Craig. You just hang in there."

"Yes, ma'am."

"Well, I've got enough to do that I'm not going to stand here and pester you, but if you need something, call me."

Craig nodded his head as Anne turned and made her way out of the backyard. He closed the gate behind her and returned to his chair. It seemed as if the noise in the surrounding yards had stopped. Then it happened again, like earlier in the day. He blinked his eyes and there he was, standing in the parking lot of The Edge. The black door opened slightly, the soft light of the bar barely penetrating the darkness of the evening. Then came the music. Johnny Cash singing about Sunday morning again.

Not yet ready to go inside, he reached into his pocket and grabbed the old flip phone. Craig twisted it, breaking it in half, then he dropped the pieces on the ground. Maybe that would be enough. He made his way to the door and, as expected, it opened. Like last time he visited, there was no couple in the booth in the far corner. As he turned his head toward the pool table, there was something almost peaceful in the way that a pool stick had been laid on the middle of the table in what looked like the middle of a game. The jukebox provided some light to the hallway leading to the restrooms and a closet. At the end of the bar was the mechanic with grease stains on his hands and forehead. He was smoking a cigarette and nursing a bottle of beer. Next to him was the lady with long brown hair and thickly applied makeup. She was wearing blue jeans and a low-cut red top that barely covered her back and stomach. She laughed heartily at whatever the man said. Kip looked perturbed when Craig turned his eyes to the bartender. On the other side of the bar was Jay. He turned his head to look toward Craig and smiled as if he was glad to see him. Craig gave him a slight nod as a courtesy. The man smiled while never breaking eye contact with Craig. Craig had to look away; it was a bit much.

It seemed as if there was nothing to do but walk over to the mechanic. He didn't feel like he was ready to talk to Kip yet. The bartender's presence was heavy and unsettling. Although Craig had stood up to him in some ways, he wasn't sure he was ready for a larger confrontation. The table was close enough to the bar where the couple was that Craig pulled out a chair and sat down. The mechanic looked over at him as he tapped his cigarette in a black ashtray and exhaled a long puff of smoke.

"What's up?" the mechanic asked after he finished exhaling. Craig caught a hint of annoyance in the man's voice, but not as intense as it had been from the man in the booth.

"Come here often?" Craig asked, then immediately felt like he had uttered a pickup line to the man and blushed.

"I guess," the mechanic replied. He looked at the woman next to him in the red top, who let out a goofy sounding laugh that lasted way longer than the joke merited.

To Craig, it felt as if the two of them were mocking him. It was almost enough to make him want to get up and leave, until he saw the mechanic shoot a quick glance at the woman that revealed anger and hatred. But before the woman turned to look at the mechanic, he looked down at his cigarette.

"Why?" Craig asked, curious about what was happening between the two.

"Because he likes the company," the woman replied as the mechanic released a lung's worth of smoke into the air. She laughed a little more as she turned and looked at him. He gave her a slight head nod but expressed no pleasure.

"I just always wind up here with her," the mechanic replied, clearly not revealing what was actually happening.

"How long have you two known each other?" Craig asked.

"Forever," the mechanic replied with a heartbreaking seriousness.

"Stop it," she said, and laughed obnoxiously again. "Twenty-seven years."

The mechanic put his head down and stared at the black ashtray in front of him. It was at this point that Craig noticed Kip had made his way over to the three of them.

"This guy bothering you?" Kip asked the mechanic.

This unsettled Craig and made him think about Kip's role in all of this. Perhaps the woman and Kip were teaming up against this poor man. The guy shook his head no, then finished off his cigarette. "If he does, you let me know. He's caused me enough trouble lately that I ought to run him out."

"Run me out?" Craig asked, confused. "I'd love for you to run me out and to never come here again."

"Hmm," Kip said with a smirk. "You ought to stick to your place. I don't need another troublemaker."

"Another?" Craig asked.

Kip ignored him and walked back toward the middle of the bar and grabbed a bottle from the shelf. Then Craig turned his gaze to Jay, who was still seated at the other end of the bar. Craig had the thought that maybe this man was the other troublemaker. The man was looking at Kip, who seemed to be avoiding eye contact with the man altogether. It was clear there was some resentment there, yet only on the man's end. Jay reached out to grab some pretzels from a basket next to him, and in doing so, Craig was once again drawn to his hand. There was something about it. It looked like a stain or maybe a scar of some sort. The smell of a freshly lit cigarette grabbed Craig's attention and brought it back to the mechanic, who was putting his lighter back into his shirt pocket and holding a freshly opened bottle of beer.

"Who is that guy?" Craig asked the two as he motioned toward Jay.

"Him? He's always here, but I don't like him," the woman said.

"Why?" Craig asked.

"I don't know. For one thing, he never drinks, which is a weird thing to do at a bar," she replied.

"Yeah, he has. Remember?" the mechanic interjected.

"Gimme a break. You talking about his story about the homemade wine?" she said dramatically, then burst out into strange laughter again.

"I like him. He seems . . ." The mechanic stopped and thought for a few seconds. "Peaceful."

"It seems like you could use some of that. Why don't you talk to him?" Craig urged, hoping to make some progress with the man and change something else up.

The mechanic looked over at the woman, then took a drink from his bottle of beer.

"He's got all he needs right here," she stated firmly as she leaned over and ran her fingers over the back of his neck.

The mechanic looked at Craig in the same way an animal in a trap might. Craig tried to get his head around what was happening. Something was off here, but he couldn't really figure it out. He looked at the woman, who was now rubbing the mechanic's shoulders and had a look in her eyes like a cat playing with a mouse that was going to be supper.

"Who are you?" Craig asked the woman. Her eyes widened, and she opened her mouth to reveal what looked like animalistic fangs. Craig could have sworn he heard a hissing noise as well. From behind her, Craig could see Kip standing there, looking on with pleasure. The woman began to look more like an animal; her skin was somewhat scaly, and there was something primal about her, like a beast on a hunt. The mechanic's face was filled with horror as he looked to Craig for some sort of hope. Craig had no idea of what to do. There was something horrific happening, and all he wanted to do was open his eyes and return to his backyard, but that wasn't in the cards. He had to face this moment. He looked around in desperation, but no one else was in the bar except Jay. He was hoping that the man would be looking at him and assessing the situation. But as he turned to look at Jay, all he could see was the back of his head.

"Sir, we could use some help," Craig uttered.

Nothing, no response.

Then, a thud.

Craig turned toward the woman to see that she had knocked the mechanic onto the ground and was now looking right at Craig, leaning forward as if she was about to pounce from her stool onto him. Kip was standing behind her, grinning from ear to ear. Whatever this was, he was loving it.

"Sir, I need help," Craig caught himself declaring loudly.

Then light appeared, bright and almost blinding.

He was back in his yard.

A New Option

"Dr. Lisa will see you now," the receptionist said in a chipper voice. It had been several days since that last trip to The Edge in his yard, and Craig was grateful that he hadn't returned there. His notepad was in his lap to remind him of everything he wanted to convey to the doctor. So much of it didn't make sense. He was hoping that she'd be able to give him some perspective. Unlike the fear he'd had with his last visit, this time, though Craig still had a bit of nervousness, there was also an excitement that he couldn't deny. For the first time in years, he felt like his life was going in a direction that would make Tabatha proud.

Craig walked through the wooden door that the young lady was holding open and made his way to Dr. Lisa's office. She was standing outside the door with a smile, motioning for him to make his way into the room.

He took a seat in the same chair from the last session, and the doctor sat across from him.

"Well, I see a notepad," she said with a smile. "I feel like that's a good sign."

"Yes, ma'am," Craig responded as he looked down at it for a moment. "I've been trying to engage with whatever is happening and trying to figure out what I'm supposed to be learning from all of it."

"Tell me what that's been like," she said in an encouraging tone.

Craig looked at his notes on the paper for a moment to refresh himself on the high points. Then he cleared his throat and began sharing. "I've learned to either break or ditch the phone in my pocket. It doesn't always work, but it usually buys me some time. I've changed the song on the jukebox, and then I go up to the people and talk to them. It seems that once I pry a bit, I can figure out why they are there, and I've been able to get them to leave. It seems like, at least for the first two instances, when I return back, the people I've talked to are gone."

"You said the first two. I'm guessing there was a third instance that was different?"

"Well, I'm not sure yet."

"What do you mean?" Dr. Lisa tilted her head in curiosity.

"I haven't been back in several days."

"Really? Has that ever happened before? Is this something new?"

"It's been slowing down since I started this. The period of time since I've been back is the longest stretch yet. I'm on new ground. I'm not sure, but maybe I won't go back. That'd be kind of weird though."

"Why is that?"

"Well, I know it sounds kind of strange, but I figured I'd have gone back at least another time or two. There were still two people there who I really haven't interacted with in those visions. I feel like I've learned some things from the others, but these two, well, they're something else."

"Tell me about what you think you've learned. Maybe reflecting on that could help you see that you've addressed or uncovered whatever you needed to."

Craig took a minute and looked back at his notepad, flipped over a few pages like he was looking for something specific, then took a deep breath and began to share. "I feel like the guy in the khaki pants, the one who always gives me dirty looks, he's who I used to be, in a way. I did a lot of things that I'm not proud of, and I hurt a lot of people.

I think that maybe I was supposed to confront that. The old biker, well, I feel like he's who I'm afraid I'll be, someone who life has passed by; there's fear there. Now that he's gone, it's in the back of my mind: Do I fall back into being this guy I used to be? It's a scary thing. Then the mechanic: He's stuck. The woman with him, she's some sort of monster, something that has control over him. I've got some of that in my life. Things I don't want to deal with that kind of have me in their grip."

"What's that in your life?" Dr. Lisa asked, looking Craig directly in his eyes.

It was too much for him to handle in the moment. He lowered his head and tried to think of some way to avoid the question. Something in him locked up. It was hard to be open like this. He didn't want anyone else to see this much of him.

"What have you got to lose?" Dr. Lisa said reassuringly as she leaned back in her chair and crossed her legs. "You wouldn't believe me if I told you some of the things that I have heard people tell me while sitting in that chair you're in right now. You know I can't tell anyone, so why not open up? We already know what it is, so just say it."

Craig looked at her and smiled slightly, leaned forward in his chair, then rubbed his forehead as he stared at the ground.

"When is the last time you had a drink?"

"Ten days." He responded so quickly that it caught him off guard.

"Not that you're counting or anything." Dr. Lisa laughed a little, and as Craig leaned back in his chair, he chuckled a little too.

"I somehow got a couple days under me, being so worked up about all of this, and I think I just realized for the first time that I couldn't dive back into it. I needed my full focus on addressing my hurt. Something seemed wrong about not facing all this with a sober mind."

"Do you want to stay that way?" Dr. Lisa asked.

"If I could."

"You can," she replied. "If you want it bad enough. I know a group that meets at a church not far from here."

Craig thought about her words and the possibility of that reality. However, what was plaguing his mind was how unresolved things felt after his last trip to The Edge. Part of him knew that staying sober was going to be dependent on dealing with whatever it was he hadn't faced yet.

"How do I go back?" Craig asked with a hint of desperation in his voice. "I need to get back there. I know I came to make it stop, but there's still something there. Something I need to figure out."

"Have you tried prayer?" Dr. Lisa asked. "Sometimes turning ourselves over to a higher power and realizing we haven't got it all figured out is the next step. Realizing we need that divine help can be a game changer. I also have some Bible study resources that I usually work through with my clients when they are ready to go a little deeper. Maybe they could help you get more comfortable with the idea of prayer."

Craig chuckled at her suggestions; he was hung up on the first one. Something about prayer scared him. It was not something he wanted to try, but in the back of his mind, he wasn't surprised that it came back to this. "I don't know about prayer, Doc. It's not really my thing," he said with a smile that let Dr. Lisa know how upset he was with this option.

"My cousin does hypnotherapy for two hundred dollars a session, but insurance doesn't cover that. My friend, prayer is a whole lot cheaper," Dr. Lisa said with a chuckle, then looked down at her hands for a few seconds.

"What do I say?" Craig asked as he thought about the option, feeling a bit childish for even considering it.

She looked back up at him and tilted her head slightly. "Just ask God to help you figure this out, to close the book on all of this."

A few moments later, the session ended, and Craig left the office, got to his car, and began his drive home, contemplating the suggestion of Dr. Lisa and becoming fearful at the thought of talking to God.

He arrived at work the next morning and was struggling a bit. He hadn't slept much the night before and had wrestled hard with the desire to drink. However, the rising sun and the humor of the men on the site was refreshing. Everyone seemed relaxed. The project was moving forward as planned, and Craig felt like he was enjoying work and not just enduring it.

When lunchtime rolled around, a few of the men headed off site to a food truck a block over; the rest went to a nearby gas station that had a deli. Craig had brought a sandwich from the house, and Jeff had some leftovers from the night before. The two men were about to sit in the shade of a tree at the edge of the site when their plans were interrupted.

"Craig, come into the trailer, please," Jackson said loudly. He always looked upset, so there was no way to determine what was happening based on the man's facial expressions.

Craig looked over to Jeff. "I'll be back. Don't eat my sandwich."

Jeff nodded with a slight smile, but both men were concerned about the security of Craig's job. He wasn't sure what he'd done wrong, but his stomach was in his throat. Jackson held the door open as Craig made his way in. The window unit in the room blasted cool air. Ordinarily, Craig would have stood in it and relaxed, but instead he sat down at the table. Jackson made his way to the other side of the room to a minifridge and opened it. "Coke or Sprite?"

The question caught Craig off guard and made him wonder about the nature of this meeting. "Uh, Sprite sounds fine. Thanks."

Jackson slid the can to him, took his hard hat off, and sat across from him. "Boy, it feels good in here."

"Yes, sir," Craig responded. "Getting pretty hot today."

"Look," Jackson said as he opened his can of Coke up. "I just wanted to thank you for putting the effort in these last several days. Often, guys get flack when they struggle but don't get recognized when they improve. I don't like harping on people, and I like to let guys know I appreciate their work."

"Thanks," Craig said. "I've been working real hard to get some stuff straight in my life."

"Well, it shows," Jackson said. "I need to go over some emails, but grab a soft drink for Jeff out there. Keep it on the down-low though. It's my personal stash."

"Yes, sir. Will do." Craig stood and grabbed a Sprite for Jeff and headed back to the tree.

He sat down on a folding chair next to Jeff, who was eating a bowl of pasta. "Here, bossman said to give this to you, but you don't know where it came from."

"Man, I thought you were going in there to get fired, and now you come out with soda?" Jeff said. "I'm impressed."

Craig began to eat his sandwich and listened to Jeff talk about family, about the job, and about other things. When a lull hit in the conversation, Craig blurted out, "What do you know about prayer?" He felt his face turn red after asking the question. It was something he had been thinking about a lot, but he hadn't intended to bring it up. It just kind of happened. Jeff must have been caught off guard, too, and choked a little on his sip of Sprite. "I'm sorry, I shouldn't have asked that. I didn't—"

"No, it's fine," Jeff responded once he stopped coughing. "I don't know. Prayer is a personal thing, you know? You can't worry about what everyone else thinks. That's what my pastor says. You just got to tell God what's on your mind and heart."

Craig was surprised by Jeff's quick response. He hadn't realized that he was a churchgoer. While he hadn't been planning on asking the first question, at this point he felt like he might as well ask another. "Do you think prayer works?"

Jeff stared off into space as he gathered his thoughts. "Yeah, I think it does. When Beth got real sick a couple of years ago, I think God healed her because we were all praying for her. When my brother died—I guess it's been five years now—I didn't really know how to get through that. He was my best friend. Prayer gave me the peace I needed."

Craig finished his lunch and watched as a few of the men made their way back to the construction site. He knew it wouldn't be long now before they'd be back to work.

"You been praying?" Jeff asked.

"No, but I've been thinking about it some."

"Well, there's one thing I know about prayer."

"What's that?"

"Don't overthink it."

CLOSING TIME

Craig sat on the old brown sectional in his living room and stared at the blank television screen. He had picked up a pizza on the way home and some root beer to go with it. He had to admit that he missed drinking a cold beer with his pizza, but ultimately, it didn't bother him that much. There was too much weighing on his mind. He'd become convinced that he needed to get back to The Edge, and at this point, he had no idea of any other way to do it. Yet the thought of trying this still scared him and made him feel strange. He had paid no mind to God for his whole life, so why in the world should God listen to him or care? Then he remembered Tabatha. She had always told him that Jesus loved him and that it didn't matter how much he had messed up; Jesus would be there for him. If only he could talk to her right now. He felt like praying would be a lot easier if she were here. He looked at the pizza on the coffee table and some uneaten crust on a plate, then closed the box and put it in the fridge, tossed the crust in the trash, and set his plate in the sink.

His plan was to turn the water on and wash the plate, but before he could do it, something in him stirred and he looked up. He cleared his throat, then spoke. "God, I don't know what I'm doing here, but if You can hear me and want to help me, I'd sure like to go back to that place one more time. I think I need to know what this all means. Amen."

It was simple but to the point. It was all he could think to do. Then he washed the plate and went back to the couch. Something in him felt more at ease, so he turned on the television and found an old movie that he liked but hadn't seen in a long time.

One moment Craig was watching a high-speed car chase, then the next he was standing outside that old familiar place. He could hear music coming through the door. As he stepped toward it, he felt around in his pocket to grab the phone. It wasn't there. Then he tried his other pocket and then his back pockets and shirt pocket, but no phone. This was different. He turned his head toward the sleepy city storefronts in the distance, and for some reason they seemed a little brighter. It was a welcome change.

His focus returned to the door, and it opened like it always had, but unlike the previous times, someone was standing there, holding it open. It was Kip. He stood face-to-face with Craig, and Craig realized how large of a man Kip was. He had never noticed how broad the man's shoulders were or the size of his arms. Kip smelled of liquor and sweat, his white shirt was yellowed, and the black apron was torn and tattered.

"Welcome back," Kip said with a smirk that made Craig uneasy. "Come and sit with me."

In a zombie-like manner, Craig followed Kip to the bar. It felt so natural and easy. Next thing he knew, a shot glass was sitting in front of him. Something about this felt both right and wrong at the same time. He put his hand to the glass, and it felt like it fit, as if it were a part of him.

"Come on, Craig. It's just for you."

While still touching the glass, Craig looked at Kip, who still had that odd smile on his face like he was in on some bad joke. "Who are you?"

"I am the one who is here to make your life a little easier and make the hard moments a little more bearable," Kip replied. "You need to quit fighting me. I know the music you like, the women you prefer, and your favorite drink. When no one else was there for you, I was. On the worst night of your life, I was the one who consoled you. Let me help you now."

Craig initially felt comforted by the words of Kip, like an old friend was talking to him. He relaxed a little and brought the glass closer, letting the smell of the whisky stir up an assortment of memories. However, it was in that moment that a new level of distrust of Kip arose in him. Anger began to rise in Craig, and his blood pressure raised as he pushed the glass away. Craig finally knew who the man was.

"You're the reason I was here that night when my phone rang and I got the most devastating news of my life," he said as he stared into the dark eyes of the barkeep. "You're the reason that I kept putting off listening to her."

"I was here for you long before Tabatha was, and now that she's gone, well, who do you have?"

"I don't like this," Craig responded. "I don't want you. We're done."

"No, we're not," Kip replied. "You can't really get away from me."

Craig, unsure of how else to prove his point, got up from the stool and looked around the bar. He realized that the music seemed off; it had become garbled and unfamiliar, as if the jukebox wasn't working right. The smoke seemed to have lifted. There was no one else there besides Kip and Jay, the mysterious man. While he wanted to talk with Jay, the jumbled music was really getting on his nerves, so he walked over to the jukebox and pounded it with his fist. Once again, Johnny Cash's familiar voice filled the air. He couldn't bear to hear the old song again. Yet a few seconds into the melody, he realized that although the voice was the same, the song was not.

Just as I am without one plea

But that my blood was shed for thee.

And that thou bidst me to come to thee.

It was familiar. He was sure he had heard it somewhere before, but he couldn't remember exactly when. It was obvious that it was some sort of church song. The lyrics felt real and hit him a bit harder than he would have liked to admit.

Then he turned from the old jukebox and scanned the bar. He could see every chair, table, and barstool from where he stood. He was expecting it to be empty, except for the man at the end of the bar, but something caught him off guard. Seated at the table closest to the door was a blonde woman, about forty, wearing a familiar blue dress, like the one Tabatha had from Dillard's, and seated across from her was Jay. They were having a conversation with each other, but Craig couldn't hear what they were saying; he was in too much disbelief. It was her. It couldn't be, but it was Tabatha.

Craig made his way to the table, hitting his knee on a chair as he walked. When she heard the noise, she turned to him and smiled.

"Tabatha?" he asked in disbelief as he pulled up a chair across from her.

"You weren't expecting me?" she asked playfully.

"No, I guess not. I-I don't know what to say," Craig blurted out. "Is this real?"

"Not in the way that you'd like for it to be, but yes. It's me. It's all the conversations we had, the things I told you, the things you know about me. All of this is to try and help you."

"You're not even here, and in some way you're trying to help me? I didn't deserve you, Tabatha. I'm so sorry."

"Why are you doing this to yourself? Why do you treat yourself the way you do?" she asked as she stared into his eyes.

"I took you for granted. I didn't listen when you tried to help me, and that night . . ." Tears began to fall. The man who had trained himself to show no emotion was now sobbing uncontrollably. It was a strange, scary feeling. As he wept, she reached over and hugged him. "I'm so sorry," he said as he melted into the feeling of being close to her again.

"I forgive you," she responded gently.

A wave of peace swept over him unlike he had ever experienced before. He felt like he had been released, freed. He looked up at her, and her own eyes were filled with tears, but a sweet smile also filled her face. "You're gonna be okay. There's someone who loves you more than you can imagine." As the words were sinking into his mind, she vanished. Part of him wanted to be upset, but he knew he couldn't be. He tried to process what she had said. The song continued playing in the background.

Just as I am, though tossed about,

With many a conflict, many a doubt,

Fightings and fears within, without,

O Lamb of God I come, I come.

He turned his eyes toward Jay, who now turned and faced Craig. He motioned with his hand for Craig to come to him, and for the first time, Craig realized who Jay really was. The man who had sat at the end of the bar so many nights was the Savior he had been curious about all these years. As Craig looked intently at Jesus, he saw that His hands were scarred from hanging on the cross—for Craig's sins, for all sins. He offered hope and a welcome presence. Craig had always imagined Jesus as being wonderful, but not someone who would have anything to do with such a messed up sinner like him. But as he walked toward Jesus, he was surprised that a nail-scarred hand stretched out to grab his own. As he took his Savior's had for the first time, he asked Jesus to forgive him and his heart turned away from the life he had been unable to leave for so long and Craig surrendered fully to Jesus. As the two headed toward the door, Craig knew through the forgiveness and power of Jesus that he'd never come back to The Edge.

A New Door

A few days later, Craig put on his best long-sleeve shirt and his favorite pair of blue jeans. He combed his hair, got in his old Camry, and drove to the church his wife had invited him to a hundred times. It was an old country church a few miles out of the city, about fifteen minutes from his home. The drive there had been peaceful; he went past the fields, away from the hustle of the city to an old, red-bricked building with white wooden doors. The gravel crunched under his Camry as he parked his car. He looked around and realized that even though some people there were dressed up, most were dressed casually like he was. An older man wore a suit, his wife a nice dress. A man wearing blue jeans and a polo had several tattoos on his arm. The man walked over to Craig as he got out of his car and shook his hand.

"How are you this morning? My name's Steve."

"Good, thank you. I'm Craig."

"Good to have you here this morning, Craig. Come on in with me."

As he walked up to the door, he could hear a song playing on the other side, singing about the love of God. The door swung open for him, feeling eerily similar to the door in his trips to The Edge. However, the elderly couple stood on the other side of the door. The man shook Craig's hand and introduced himself while the elderly woman stared at him. "What did you say your name was?"

"I'm Craig Brown," he responded.

"Your wife was Tabatha!" the woman declared.

"Yes ma'am," Craig replied, confused as to how she knew this.

"Your wife told me all about you. She used to come to Bible study with me." She opened up an old black Bible and pulled out a piece of paper revealing a list of about ten names. "This is my prayer list, and I've been praying for you for a long time. Tabatha loved you so much, and she sure wanted you to know that Jesus loves you too. Do you know that Jesus loves you?"

Once again, his eyes started watering up. The woman and her husband gave Craig a look offering encouragement and hope.

"Yes, ma'am, I think I'm starting to realize that."

Thank You for Reading *The Edge*

The Edge is the story of one man finding hope in Christ Jesus. Just as Craig came to a place where he realized he was lost in his sin and struggles—and that he couldn't fix it on his own—we, too, must recognize that our sin separates us from God.

The good news is that in His deep love for us, God sent His own Son, Jesus Christ, to live a perfect life and die on the cross for our sins. If we're willing to acknowledge our need for the forgiveness that only He can offer, turn from our sins, and surrender our lives to Him, we can find the true and lasting hope that only Christ provides.

It can be as simple as praying a prayer like this: "Dear God, I know that I am a sinner, and my sin separates me from You. I ask for the forgiveness of my sins through the death and resurrection of Jesus. I turn from those sins and give You my life. In Jesus' name I pray, amen."

WANT TO READ MORE?

If you enjoyed the message found in *The Edge*, would you consider leaving a review and rating it on Amazon? Your support means so much.

I'm currently developing more novellas in the *Stories of Hope* series. You can also check out my full-length novel, **Bayou Refuge**—an inspirational Christian mystery where nothing is quite what it seems. It's available now on Amazon.

To stay connected, I'd love to hear from you. Join my Facebook community: **Joshua Powell: Author Page**.

About the Author

Joshua Powell is the pastor of First Baptist Church of Bogalusa, Louisiana, and a graduate of New Orleans Baptist Theological Seminary. He was born and raised in Louisiana and loves writing stories that reflect both the grit and grace of real life.

He is the author of *Bayou Refuge*, an inspirational Christian mystery, and *The Edge*, the first novella in his Stories of Hope series.

You can connect with Joshua and learn more about upcoming books by visiting his Facebook page: **Joshua Powell – Author Page**.

Bayou Refuge

Check out *Bayou Refuge* an inspirational Christian mystery by Joshua Powell.

After nearly a decade, Charles, a small-town Louisiana pastor, finds himself back at Bayou Refuge, an old church campground and conference center that's been closed for years. He's been invited to lead a special event for people who are curious about what it means to know God. Even though he's surrounded by familiar faces, Charles begins to realize that everything is not as it seems. Soon it becomes clear that the conversations that Charles will have with these people about God may be the final conversation of their lives. As Charles wrestles with the seriousness of this responsibility, he must also consider what it means to trust God to the very end.

Available now on Amazon in paperback, ebook, on Kindle Unlimited and as an Audiobook. Come Visit the Bayou.

BAYOU
REFUGE
If this was your last conversation…
if you only had one chance…
what would you say?
JOSHUA POWELL

Coming October 2025

The Second *Stories of Hope* Novella